CW00847198

For Janice and Adrienne

xx

For more books by Allan visit www.allanplenderleith.com



This edition first published 2013
by Ravette Publishing Limited
PO Box 876, Horsham, West Sussex RH12 9GH



ISBN: 978-1-84161-371-0

by Allan Plenderleith

RAVETTE PUBLISHING

**Far** far away on a tumbledown farm lives a little brown chicken called

Flo.

Every chicken on the farm lays one egg every day.

All
except
Flo.

Flo tried everything to help her lay an egg.

But **nothing** worked.

One day the rain came.

The other chickens fled to the coop.
But there was no room for Flo.

So she hid
under a tree.

But as the rain fell
so did something else...

The next morning, the sun was shining.

When Flo woke up
she got quite a
surprise.

EGG!
EGG! MY VERY OWN EGG!

The other chickens thought the egg looked strange.

But Flo **loved** the egg more than anything in the **world**.

She cared for her egg all through the year.

Every egg on the farm
hatched...

All

except

Flo's.

But that night
a dark thing
came.

All the other chickens fled to the coop.

All

except

Flo.

It crept towards Flo and her egg.

Suddenly,
it pounced

knocking Flo
into a tree.

Egg!
Egg!
My very
own egg!

But it did not
want Flo's egg.
It wanted
Flo.

Suddenly, it
jumped at Flo
snapping its
slobbery
jaws!

But then
something
incredible
happened...

cRaCk!

cRaaCkKcK!!

SON! SON!
MY VERY
OWN SON!

Flo's son grabbed the dark thing by the tail...

And threw him far far away…

And the farm was safe
forever more thanks to
Flo and her very own son.

the end.

Also available as an app for iPhone, iPad HD and Android devices.

Other books by Allan Plenderleith:

allanplenderleith.com